PAUL BOROVSKY
GEORGE

 Greenwillow Books, New York

THE FULL-COLOR ARTWORK WAS DONE
WITH BLACK PEN, WATERCOLORS, AND
COLORED PENCILS.
THE TEXT TYPE IS ITC VELJOVIC.

A DIVISION OF WILLIAM MORROW & COMPANY, INC.,
105 MADISON AVENUE, NEW YORK, N.Y. 10016.
PRINTED IN SINGAPORE BY TIEN WAH PRESS
FIRST EDITION   10 9 8 7 6 5 4 3 2 1

LIBRARY OF CONGRESS CATALOGING-IN-PUBLICATION DATA
BOROVSKY, PAUL.
GEORGE / BY PAUL BOROVSKY.
P.   CM.
SUMMARY: HAVING BECOME EDUCATED WHILE ATTENDING
SCHOOL WITH HIS MASTER, A DOG IN TURN EDUCATES HIS
ZOO ANIMAL FRIENDS UNTIL HE DEVELOPS A YEARNING
TO TRAVEL AND LEARN MORE.
ISBN 0-688-09150-4.
ISBN 0-688-09151-2 (LIB. BDG.)
[1. DOGS—FICTION.   2. ZOO ANIMALS—FICTION.]
I. TITLE   PZ7.B64849GE 1990
[E]—DC19   89-2022   CIP   AC

FOR SUSY

Peter lived in a small zoo with his grandfather the zookeeper, and his dog, George.

Peter and George were best friends and went everywhere together. Every morning, with their sacks of books, Peter and George would walk briskly to the schoolhouse.

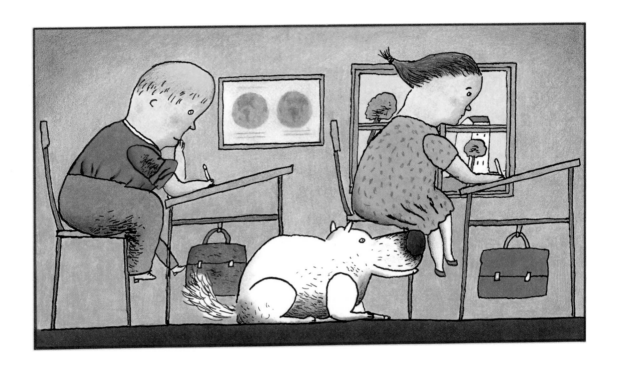

George loved school and was a good student. His favorite subjects were geography and mathematics.

Every day George and Peter would study together, and soon George became the most educated dog in the country. So it was not at all surprising when one day he began to talk. "Don't tell anyone yet," he said to Peter.

After school, George would visit his friends in the zoo
and teach them what he had learned.

One morning Grandfather brought the elephant his breakfast.

"Ho hum, grass again," sighed the elephant.

Grandfather jumped back in surprise. "He spoke! The elephant spoke!" he cried. "But that can't be! Elephants can't talk!"

Nevertheless, Grandfather rushed back to his house to
tell Peter what had happened.

"Good morning, good morning!" screamed the monkeys.

"What's your hurry?" growled the bear.

"You forgot to feed me," croaked the alligator.

"Just where do you think you are running to?"
 roared the lion.

Grandfather burst open the door. "They're talking, the animals are talking!" he gasped. Peter looked at George and smiled.

"Don't you believe me?" asked Grandfather.

"Of course we believe you." It was George who replied.

"You can talk, too!" exclaimed Grandfather.

"Why, I'm the one who taught the animals everything they know," said George.

"That's wonderful!" Grandfather said, beginning to smile.

"Now the animals can tell us when they want something." And all three danced around the room for joy.

George decided to open a school right in the zoo. He was a skillful teacher and loved his job. The animals were thrilled with their new school, and they lined up every morning waiting for George to open the doors.

The day began with a singing class. The birds, who were the best singers, led the class. And although at times the snakes had difficulty keeping in tune, they all enjoyed the class tremendously.

Geography was the giraffe's favorite subject. He would draw maps on the blackboard of the places he wanted to visit.

The owl was good at math, and was the first to answer the difficult problems.

The day ended with a dancing class. The bears were impressive dancers, and were often asked by the others to perform.

One day, as Grandfather was clearing the table after dinner, he saw that George had not touched his food. "Something is most definitely wrong," he thought. George loved spinach pie, and usually had two helpings.

Peter had also noticed that George was not his usual self.
He seemed very quiet, and at night he sat in his room
staring at the stars.

George finally told Grandfather and Peter what was troubling him. "I'm afraid it's time for me to leave," he said.

"But why?" asked Peter.

"I've taught the animals everything I can," said George. "I want to travel and learn about different places and things."

"But we will miss you so much!" said Peter.

"Don't worry," said George, "I will be back. And in the meantime, I will write often."

With a small sack on his back, George set off
on his journey.

He kept his promise and wrote almost every week. The
giraffe drew a big map and tracked George's journey on it.

Peter read his letters out loud to all the animals.

And after many, many months, the letter
they were all waiting for finally came.
George was coming home.